REGULAR SHOW™

TALES FROM REGULAR SHOW
BY JAKE BLACK

PSS!
PRICE STERN SLOAN
An Imprint of Penguin Group (USA) LLC

PRICE STERN SLOAN
Published by the Penguin Group
Penguin Group (USA) LLC, 375 Hudson Street,
New York, New York 10014, USA

USA | Canada | UK | Ireland | Australia
New Zealand | India | South Africa | China

penguin.com
A Penguin Random House Company

Illustrated by Dave Mottram.

Photo credit: cover and page 1: © Oleg Shipov/iStock/Thinkstock.

Published in 2014 by Price Stern Sloan, a division of Penguin Young
Readers Group, 345 Hudson Street, New York, New York 10014. *PSS!* is a
registered trademark of Penguin Group (USA) LLC. Manufactured in China.

ISBN 978-0-8431-8052-7   10 9 8 7 6 5 4 3 2 1

"Dude! Dude! Duuuuude!" Rigby yelled as he ran inside the house.

Rigby's best buddy, Mordecai, was sitting on the couch watching TV and totally ignoring him. Rigby jumped in front of the TV and started waving his arms wildly.

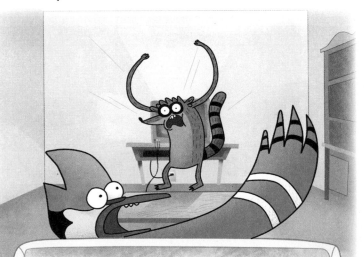

"Dude, what the *H*?" Mordecai said.

"Biggest. News. Ever," Rigby answered. Mordecai didn't even look up. He bobbed his head from side to side, trying to see what was on the TV screen behind his bud. Rigby repositioned himself right in front of his friend's face. "Dude, are you even listening to me?!"

"Obviously not," Mordecai answered.

Rigby grabbed the remote and turned off the TV.

"Hey! What gives?" Mordecai said.

"Relax, man. This is seriously huge news. Trust me," Rigby said excitedly. "You know how every year they do that Arts in the Park thing, where they put on some boring play or something? Well, you'll never believe who's starring in the play this year!"

Mordecai shrugged his shoulders. He knew about the play. Every summer, the city put on a bunch of plays, orchestra concerts, and other boring stuff like that. And the worst part about it was that he and Rigby would have to do some actual work. It was their job to build the stage, set up chairs, and make sure there were enough food stands and Porta Potties for all the guests.

"Who?" Mordecai asked dryly.

"Bill Carpenter!" Rigby announced.

Mordecai shrugged again. "So?"

"So? So?!" Rigby couldn't believe his ears. "He's only the greatest actor who has ever lived! And he's coming here, to the Park!"

Mordecai got off the couch and walked toward the kitchen. "Bill Carpenter is *not* the greatest actor who ever lived. In fact, he's really pretty terrible. I heard he has the worst memory ever, and can't ever remember his lines. Shooting the show takes a million times longer than it needs to. Nobody likes him. Well, except about a million stupid *Star Warriors* fans."

Rigby gritted his teeth. This was the most insulting thing he'd ever heard. "He *is* great! He was the first general in the whole Star Warriors franchise! And he's coming here! And I'm going to meet him!"

Mordecai reached into the fridge and pulled out a can of soda. "Still not the greatest actor. Besides, like Benson would let you meet him. Staff isn't supposed to 'cavort with the talent,' remember?"

Rigby's face fell. He'd forgotten all about Benson's "no cavorting" rule.

"Maybe he'll make an exception, just this once. I *have* to meet him!"

"No," said Benson, sternly. "No one gets to meet the actors. You know the rules. And Mr. Carpenter requested a bodyguard to make sure no crazy lunatics like you two harass him. Now get back to work. The stage needs to be set up for this evening's performance."

Benson peeled away in his golf cart. Rigby and Mordecai stared at the massive stage sitting in pieces in front of them. *They* needed to put *this* together?!

"Stupid Benson!" Rigby yelled. "Stupid stage!" Then he kicked a pile of iron support beams as hard as he could.

"Ow! Ow! Ow!" Rigby yelled, hopping around on one foot.

"Chill, dude. You're kind of proving Benson's point. Why would Bill Carpenter *want* to meet a lunatic like you?" Mordecai said.

Rigby sighed, but didn't answer Mordecai. There had to be a way that he could meet his hero. He sighed again.

Just as Rigby was about to help Mordecai lift a support beam into position, the two friends heard the roar of a convoy of engines. Entering the Park were several trailers and tour buses carrying the actors for the play. The buses stopped across the Park. Rigby could see Benson driving his golf cart up to the bus marked MR. CARPENTER and begin to speak with the tour manager.

"Stupid Benson," Rigby said again.

A couple hours later, Rigby and Benson only had gotten the stage about a third of the way set up. That was a *lot* of work for them—time for a well-deserved break!

"Come with me," Rigby said. He had a plan.

"Sure." Mordecai shrugged his shoulders. "But where?"

Rigby turned away from Mordecai. "Ummmm . . . now where . . . ," he said, more to himself than to Mordecai. He started to walk across the Park toward the tour buses.

Mordecai raced after him. "Dude, this is a bad idea.

Benson will totally fire you if he catches you bugging Mr. Carpenter in his bus."

"I don't care, Mordecai. Ever since I was little, Bill Carpenter has been my hero. This is my only chance to see him live and in person! And I need your help," Rigby said, more determined than ever.

Before they knew it, the duo was just outside the circle of tour buses. Rigby walked on his tippy-toes, trying to sneak as close to Carpenter's bus as he could.

"Uh-oh. Mega problem," Mordecai whispered. Rigby stopped dead in his tracks.

"What?" Rigby asked, panic in his voice. Mordecai pointed to the front of the bus, near the door. "You gotta be kidding me," Rigby whispered.

Muscle Man was standing next to Carpenter's bus, wearing an ID tag around his neck that said BODYGUARD. Wait—Muscle Man was Carpenter's bodyguard?!

"Crap," Rigby said.

"If Muscle Man sees you, you're definitely fired," Mordecai said.

"Stupid Muscle Man," Rigby kicked the tire of the tour bus and started the long walk back to the stage setup. But he had gotten only a few feet when something stopped him. He could hear a faint cry for help coming from one of the tour buses.

"You hear that?" Rigby asked. He and Mordecai paused, listening.

"Help . . . ," the cry came again.

"That's coming from Carpenter's bus," Mordecai said. But he didn't need to—Rigby already was on his way to the back of the bus, out of Muscle Man's sight.

"Gimme a boost," Rigby said to Mordecai. Before

Mordecai could crouch down to lift his friend, Rigby already was climbing up onto his shoulders. From his position on the top of Mordecai's shoulders, Rigby was able to peek into one of the bus's tinted windows.

Rigby pressed his face onto the glass. He could see his hero, crouched in a ball, on the ground next to a wall.

"Help . . . ," Carpenter repeated.

"No way," Rigby said.

"What?" Mordecai gasped from below, his knees

starting to buckle under Rigby's weight.

"Carpenter wears a toupee! I'd heard the rumors, but . . ."

"Is that why he needs help?" Mordecai asked through gritted teeth.

"Oh. Right. Sorry," Rigby said, refocusing. He tapped on Carpenter's window. "Hello, Mr. Carpenter? Why do you need help?"

The window cracked open, and Bill Carpenter peered out. "My bodyguard won't let me out of my trailer. I'm a prisoner in my own bus!"

Rigby grinned from ear to ear. "No problem. We'll help you get out. Remember, 'unity is the force by which prosperity comes'!"

"Uh . . . what?" Carpenter asked.

"'Unity is the force by which prosperity comes' . . . from *Star Warriors*. Your catchphrase!" Rigby said.

"Oh right. Of course," Carpenter said. "I forgot. Can you please help me get out of here?"

"You got it!" Rigby said.

"How are you going to do that?" Mordecai asked, as Rigby climbed off his shoulders.

"I've got a plan," Rigby smiled. "Follow me."

This was the best job Muscle Man had ever had. He was born to be a bodyguard. No one would get into or out of Bill Carpenter's bus without going through Muscle Man first, and no one could get through him. So he was *really* surprised when he saw Mordecai walking toward him.

"Muscle Man, Benson told me to come get you. We need your help with the stage setup," Mordecai said.

"What? I'm supposed to be here guarding Bill Carpenter. I ain't going to help with no stage setup," Muscle Man grunted.

"No, it's cool. Benson said no one's going to bother Mr. Carpenter, because everyone knows they'll get fired if they do. Plus, you're the only one around here who's strong enough to lift the support beams, because they weigh, like, infinity pounds," Moredcai explained. "It'll only take a minute."

Muscle Man thought for a second and said, "Okay. Let's go throw around some steel! Yeah!"

Muscle Man and Mordecai walked away from the bus, toward the stage setup. Rigby tiptoed around to the bus door and gave it a push.

"Dang it. Locked," Rigby said. "Time for plan B."

He picked up a rock tied on the end of a rope and swung it over his shoulder and toward the bus. The rock sailed toward one of the bus windows, shattering it. Luckily, the rock wrapped around a leg of one of the seats inside the bus, so Rigby grabbed the rope and started to climb in.

"My name is Rigby. I've come to rescue you," he

declared to Mr. Carpenter as soon as he got inside the
bus. Carpenter was busy making some last-minute
adjustments to his toupee.

"Thank you! I've been trapped in here so long,
I can't remember what the outside world's like,"
Carpenter said.

"Heh, heh, good one," Rigby said.

Rigby grabbed Carpenter around the waist. "I'll
help you climb out," Rigby said as he attempted to
pull Carpenter near the broken window.

"No, you won't! I won't let you kidnap me!"
Carpenter said, shoving Rigby through the window
to the ground outside. Rigby landed with a thud and
a grunt. Carpenter used the rope to rappel down the
side of the bus, all the way to the ground.

"Hey, what gives?" Rigby said as he stood up.

"What do you mean?" Carpenter responded, a
blank expression on his face.

"You pushed me through the window!" Rigby said.

"I did? I'm sorry. I just knew I had to escape from
the bus."

Across the Park, Muscle Man hefted the final

support beam into position. The stage was almost ready. After he admired his handiwork, his eyes drifted back toward Carpenter's bus.

"Hey! You can't do that!" Muscle Man yelled at Rigby and Carpenter. He ran at them, screaming.

"Gotta go," Rigby said. He grabbed Carpenter by the hand and pulled him behind the bus where the cart was still running, waiting for them to make their getaway. The duo jumped into the cart and drove as fast as they could across the Park, away from the buses and Muscle Man.

"What are you doing?!" Carpenter yelled.

"Rescuing you," Rigby said, focused.

Meanwhile, Muscle Man was gaining on them. "I'll get you both," he screamed as he ran.

"No, you won't," Rigby muttered.

"Are you crazy? This isn't what I wanted at all!" Carpenter screamed.

Rigby turned the wheel hard to the right, turning the cart back toward the stage area. He pressed the accelerator all the way down—pushing the cart to its limits, surpassing ten miles an hour.

Muscle Man saw where the cart was headed and changed his course to match. In a matter of seconds, he'd caught up to the cart and wrapped his massive arms around Rigby's head and covered Rigby's eyes with his giant hands.

"Whoa, dude, I can't see!" Rigby yelled.

"You can't kidnap Mr. Carpenter on my watch!" Muscle Man yelled.

"Mr. Carpenter's outta here," Carpenter said, diving from his seat in the cart to the ground and rolling to safety on the grass. He ran away from the cart, racing into a wooded part of the Park.

Muscle Man and Rigby wrestled in the cart, causing it to swerve and bobble around. Muscle Man tried shoving Rigby out of the thing, but that scrappy raccoon wouldn't budge.

"Rigby! Muscle Man!" Mordecai yelled from across the Park. The two stopped wrestling in the cart and turned just in time to see a tree directly in front of them. Rigby tried slamming on the brakes, but it was too late. The cart crashed into the tree, throwing Rigby and Muscle Man through the air. Then they landed with a giant *SMASH!* on the ground.

Mordecai caught up to them.

"Bad news: Carpenter's gone," Mordecai said. "He ran into the woods."

"I'm sure he'll be back," Rigby said.

"Yeah, but what if Benson finds him first?" Mordecai asked.

Muscle Man and Rigby looked at each other, realizing they'd both be in huge trouble if Benson found Mr. Carpenter first.

Bill Carpenter strolled through the woods, happy and calm. He'd rarely seen so beautiful a day or so great a place as this. It was sunny, and there were lots of trees. He had no idea where he was or how he'd gotten there, but that didn't matter. It was pretty.

He sat down to pet a squirrel. He patted its back, and the little animal scampered away.

"Good-bye, little fella!" Carpenter said cheerfully. He was so happy being in the woods that he

didn't hear Mordecai, Rigby, and Muscle Man calling for him.

"Mr. Carpenter! Come back!" Rigby yelled.

Muscle Man pulled a tree up by its roots and looked in the hole below. "You down there, Mr. Carpenter?"

In the distance, the trio heard laughter that sounded a lot like Carpenter's.

"You hear that?" Mordecai asked his friends.

"Yeah! He's this way," Rigby said, running deeper into the woods.

In a few short minutes, the gang found Carpenter under a tree, smelling a flower.

"Hello! Beautiful day," Carpenter said.

"Uh . . . yeah . . . hi," Rigby replied.

Mordecai stood over Carpenter. "Mr. Carpenter, you've got to go back. Pretty soon it'll be time for the play."

Mr. Carpenter looked up at Mordecai, confused. "Play?"

"Yeah, the play you're performing in tonight. Don't you remember?" Rigby said.

"I'm afraid I don't," Carpenter said. "But, I don't want to do a play. It's too pretty here.

"You're an actor who can't remember things? How do you learn your lines and stuff?" Mordecai asked, exasperated.

"Oh, that's easy. My agent and manager put cue cards all over the set for me to find and read. But I'm not performing tonight."

Carpenter jumped to his feet and began to run. "You can't catch me!"

"We don't have time for this!" Muscle Man said, annoyed.

Muscle Man tackled Carpenter, and lifted him up off the ground. Muscle Man threw the actor over his shoulder and carried him out of the woods. Rigby and Mordecai followed them.

"Wheeeeee!" Carpenter squealed as Muscle Man carried him quickly through the woods.

As the group stepped out of the trees, they were met by an angry Benson.

"Crap," Rigby said.

The play performance that night was excellent.

Mr. Carpenter read his hidden cue cards and performed brilliantly. By the time the gang got back to the main Park, he'd forgotten about being in the woods and wanted to perform the play. But Rigby and Mordecai didn't get to see it. At least not from the seating area. They were assigned to pick up all the trash left by the audience.

"I hope you're happy. We've got, like, a year's worth garbage duty because you *had* to meet Bill Carpenter," Mordecai said, annoyed.

"Totally worth it," Rigby said. The tour buses were packed up and pulling away after the play. Rigby just stared at Carpenter's bus with a giant grin on his face as it pulled out of the Park. "Totally worth it."

DATE NIGHT

"This is a terrible idea, guys," Benson said. "I hate blind dates. And meeting people on the Internet? I don't know. It sounds ridiculous."

Mordecai and Rigby smirked at each other.

"It's all good, Benson. You need to get out more. Meet the ladies. Have fun once in a while," Mordecai reassured his boss.

"You know how to have fun, right, Benson?" Rigby asked. Mordecai shot him a look that said, "shut up."

Benson sighed, hovered his mouse over the SEND button, and clicked it. A week after creating an online-dating profile, he had just sent an email confirming a blind date with a mystery woman—a woman he was going to meet later that very night. Benson was super-duper nervous. He wasn't much of a dater, and he didn't love meeting new people, especially new people he was supposed to date. But Mordecai and Rigby had convinced him that he needed to give it a try. After all, they knew how to have fun better than anyone else.

The computer let out a *ding*, notifying the group that Benson's email had been received by the mystery woman. He knew her name was Sylvia and that she had blond hair and a big smile. She lived with her family in the suburbs not far from the Park.

"Hey, she looks nice enough," Mordecai said,

looking at her picture again.

"I guess." Benson shrugged, his heart completely not in this.

"What's your activity?" Rigby asked. This dating site didn't just match you with someone—it planned your whole date for you, too!

Benson scrolled down to the bottom of the page and when he found his date for the night, his face fell. "Art-museum opening gala," he read aloud.

"Bahahahahahahahahaha!" Mordecai and Rigby laughed.

"I knew this was a terrible idea." Benson glared at them. "I'm not going."

Mordecai and Rigby stopped laughing. "You can't back out now, Benson. Sylvia's planning on it!" Mordecai said seriously.

"Black-tie event . . .," Benson read from the screen. "Ah, man! I have to wear a tuxedo?"

"That means Sylvia will be wearing an evening gown. She'll be beautiful," Mordecai promised.

"I have to pick her up at her parents' house!" Benson shrieked in horror. "I don't want to meet her parents! This is going way too fast."

Mordecai put his hand on Benson's back. "It's just a safety thing. No bigs. They just need to make sure you're not a serial killer or something."

Benson glanced up at Mordecai. "I hope you're right about all this, Mordecai. If you're not, you're going to clean the off-leash dog area permanently."

Mordecai swallowed hard. "You'll have fun."

"Heh. Art museum," Rigby snickered.

Benson stood in front of the mirror. He was lucky—his old tuxedo still fit. He also was lucky because Pops knew how to tie a bow tie.

"If it is not hand-tied, it shan't be worn," Pops said as he maneuvered the black tie around Benson's neck. Benson looked at himself in the mirror one last time, gave the bow tie a little tug and headed out the door.

Benson drove his car to Sylvia's house and pulled into the driveway. It was a nice-looking house, not too big and not too small. It seemed like a place where normal people lived.

Still, Benson was nervous. He grabbed a small bouquet of the flowers he had pulled from the ground at the Park before leaving for his date, walked up to the front door, and knocked. A small boy opened the door.

"Uh, hey, kid. Is,

uh, Sylvia here?" Benson stammered.

"Sylvia!" the kid yelled, throwing the door open.
"Some guy with a giant gumball-machine head is here
for you!"

Benson tentatively stepped through the front
door and into the living room of Sylvia's house. He
was met by twenty-five sets of eyes—Sylvia's entire
family!

"Uh, hello . . . ," Benson said to no one in particular.

"So, you must be Benson," a large man said gruffly.

"Yup . . ." Benson gulped.

"I'm Sylvia's father. What are your intentions toward my daughter?"

Benson's eyes darted around the room. Everyone was staring at him with the same intense look that Sylvia's big scary father had on his face.

"Just . . . uh . . . a . . . date . . . ," Benson said, staring at the carpet.

"Oh, don't listen to him," a kind-looking woman said. "I'm Sylvia's mother. And this, as you probably figured out, is her family. Her whole family. Her grandparents, Joe and Georgianna."

The grandparents glared at Benson.

"Her uncles, Stevie and

Winston—they're cops."

"So don't try anything, or we'll come down on you with the full force of the law!" Uncle Stevie said by way of his greeting. Benson's eyes grew wide. He wasn't sure if Uncle Stevie was kidding.

"Sylvia's six brothers, who are all master ninjas." Sylvia's mother gestured toward a group of six terrifyingly large men who each snapped into an attack pose.

"And the rest are cousins," Sylvia's mother said, smiling. The large family glared at Benson.

Sylvia, dressed in a beautiful evening gown, finally entered the room. "Hi, Benson!" she said very excitedly. "Are you ready to go?"

"Absolutely!" Benson said, and he started to run for the door.

"Wait for me, silly!" Sylvia called out. Benson stopped in his tracks and glanced over his shoulder, a tad annoyed at her delay. He couldn't wait to get out of that nuthouse!

"Bye, Daddy," Sylvia said, as she kissed her father on the cheek.

"You better be home by ten," her father replied, burning a hole through Benson with his glare. "Or else . . ."

"Oh, Daddy," Sylvia said with a laugh. Benson gulped. It was going to be a long night.

Benson pulled up to the Art Museum valet-parking area and got out of the car. He handed his car keys to the valet without looking at him. "Don't wreck it," he said.

"Of course, sir," the valet answered, his voice very familiar. Benson finally looked at him. It was Mordecai!

"What are you doing here?" Benson hissed.

"Dude, I don't want to clean the stupid dog park. That's just sick. We got your back tonight," Mordecai whispered.

"You better," Benson said, as he opened the

passenger-side door for Sylvia. Benson took her hand, and they walked into the Art Museum.

The gala was set up beautifully. There were a whole bunch of awesome paintings hanging on the walls, of course, and a ton of cool statues standing behind red velvet ropes. In the center of the room was an ice sculpture of a giant seagull flying over a punch bowl filled with water and lemon slices.

Several waiters walked around the museum carrying trays of hors d'oeuvres and sandwiches with little plastic toothpicks stuck in them.

Hmmm . . . nice setup. This may not be so bad after all, Benson thought.

Rigby, dressed as a waiter, approached the pair. "Sandwiches?" he offered in his best waiter voice.

Benson and Sylvia each selected a sandwich and munched on them as they stared at a giant painting on the far wall.

"I bit off part of my toothpick and swallowed it," Sylvia said.

Nope, never mind. This is just as bad as I thought it would be, Benson thought.

"I'll get you a drink," Benson said to Sylvia. He moved quickly to the center table and its crystal punch bowl filled with water and fancy lemon slices. He grabbed Rigby by the arm, dragging him along.

"This girl is so not my type, Rigby! She ate a toothpick. What am I going to do?" Benson asked, panicking.

"Relax, Benson. It'll all be over soon," Rigby replied.

"And you'll be cleaning up dog doo for the rest of your life!"

Benson stormed back to his date, water in hand. Sylvia took a drink from the cup.

"Mmmmmm! This is good! What is it?" Sylvia asked, way too excitedly.

"Uh . . . water . . . ," Benson muttered quietly.

"Oh! Ha-ha! Silly me. I thought it was just really watered-down lemonade," Sylvia laughed.

Benson rolled his eyes. Sylvia, not noticing Benson's irritation, grabbed him around the arms and pulled him in for a tight hug.

"Kiss me, big boy!" Sylvia yelled. Benson struggled, trying free himself from her kung-fu grip.

"Yeah-yuh! Get some, Benson!" Mordecai called from across the room.

Benson wrestled his arms free and shoved Sylvia away. Her family's warnings of "Don't try anything . . . ," "Be home by ten . . . ," and "The full force of the law . . ." danced through his gumball-machine-shaped head.

"No! I'm not going to kiss you! I don't even like you!" Benson hollered.

Sylvia's eyes filled with tears. "You—you're not going to kiss me?"

"No. I already said that!" Benson said.

Sylvia's tears dried up. Her sadness suddenly turned to rage. Sylvia's body started to shake . . . and grow . . . and grow . . . and turn . . . green? Pillars of fire shot out of her nose, and torched a couple paintings across the room.

"Oh no," Benson muttered.

Sylvia grew even bigger and smashed through the ceiling of the museum. Sylvia was no longer a pretty blonde with a big smile—she was a giant troll! All the other gala attendees started to scream and flee the building.

"Kiss me!" roared Troll-Sylvia.

"Ha! Benson totally met a troll on the Internet!

Get it?" Rigby laughed.

"Guys!" Benson yelled. "A little help here!"

Rigby pulled as many of the toothpicks as he could get his hands on out of the sandwiches and threw them at the she-troll. The toothpicks just bounced off her tough skin.

"Aw, man. Fail!" Rigby yelled to Benson. "Sorry, dude!"

Troll-Sylvia swung her massive arms at the center table, shattering the ice sculpture, and obliterating the table.

Just then, Mordecai crashed Benson's car through the museum's entrance, speeding toward Troll-Sylvia. "Not my car, Mordecai!" Benson yelled.

"Only way, dude!" Mordecai yelled back, as he jumped from the car just as it smashed into Troll-Sylvia's leg in a fiery explosion.

"Kiss me!" Troll-Sylvia roared louder.

Mordecai and Rigby stood next to Benson, who was trembling with fear.

"I think you need to kiss her," Mordecai whispered.

"But I don't want to," Benson said stubbornly. "Especially now. Sick. She doesn't look anything like her picture!"

"Do you want to live? 'Cause I think kissing her's the only way that's gonna happen," Rigby shot back.

Benson looked up Troll-Sylvia. He knew Rigby was right.

"Sylvia? I was only kidding. I'll kiss you!" Benson yelled.

Troll-Sylvia reached out a claw and grabbed Benson. She pulled him up to her giant dragon face. Benson closed his eyes tight, puckered his lips, and leaned into the ugly troll face. He kissed a quick peck on her troll mouth.

In an instant, bolts of electricity, fire, and colorful beams of light and energy surrounded both Benson and Troll-Sylvia as she returned to her human form. Sylvia grinned from ear to ear.

"This was the best date ever, Benson!" Sylvia exclaimed.

Mordecai and Rigby were shocked.

Benson glared at them. "You bring the cart?" Benson demanded.

"Yeah," said Mordecai.

"Good. You're taking us home," Benson ordered.

The cart, loaded with Mordecai, Rigby, Sylvia, and Benson, approached Sylvia's house, where Sylvia's entire family stood in the front yard waiting for them. Sylvia stepped out of the car and waved good-bye to the boys.

"Thank you for a wonderful evening, Benson! Call me!" Sylvia said.

"Benson!" Sylvia's dad yelled from the porch. "It's ten-oh-one."

"Yikes," Benson whispered. "Floor it, Mordecai!"

IDENTITY THEFT

After a long day of almost working, Mordecai and Rigby loved to go to the Coffee Shop to relax. They especially liked it when Margaret and Eileen were working there.

"Hey, Eileen, is Margaret working tonight?" Mordecai asked as he and Rigby settled into their usual table.

"Yeah, but she doesn't want to see you after what you said this morning," Eileen said curtly.

Mordecai and Rigby shot each other a confused look.

"Wait, what? What did I say?" Mordecai asked.

Eileen glared at him, "If you have to ask, it's even worse! I don't want to talk to you, either!"

Eileen stormed off, leaving Mordecai and Rigby alone and without their coffee.

"Do you still want to talk to me?" Rigby called after her. "Eileen? Hello?"

"Let's go, dude," Mordecai said. "Obviously something is up."

As they were leaving, Mordecai pulled out his phone, and noticed that he'd sent Margaret a text message earlier that day. He opened the message and let out a super-loud gasp.

"Dude, check it," Mordecai said, holding the phone so Rigby could read the text.

"'Margaret, you're fat and stupid. Mordecai,'" Rigby read. "Dude, harsh! Why would you say that?"

Mordecai threw up his hands, totally frustrated. "I didn't! That's the point! Someone must've stolen my phone or something."

Rigby looked perplexed. "When? We were together all day, and there was nobody around who could've stolen your phone. Except me, I guess."

Mordecai glared at Rigby. He couldn't believe it. "Did you send this text to Margaret?!"

"Are you serious?" Rigby threw back. "I wouldn't do that. After everything I did to get her to like you?! C'mon, man!"

Mordecai shook his head. Rigby might have exaggerated his part in helping Mordecai get together with Margaret, but Mordecai knew he wouldn't have sent the text to her.

"I gotta get this figured out, or Margaret's never gonna speak to me again," Mordecai said sadly.

The next morning, Mordecai and Rigby met with Benson to get their work assignments for the day, just like they did every day. Today was different, though. There was tension in the air. Benson seemed extra grouchy.

"You think you're funny, Mordecai?" Benson demanded, out of nowhere.

Mordecai shrugged his shoulders. "Yeah, sometimes, I guess."

Benson stood up from his desk, livid. "You want to 'chew up my head and spit me out on the Park sidewalk so people can step on me and mess up my gumballs and the Park all at the same time'?"

"Uh . . . what? No!" Mordecai replied.

Benson shook his head in disbelief. "Well, then how do you explain the email you sent me?!"

"I didn't send you an email," Mordecai said.

"Yes, you did. It's right here." Benson turned his computer screen around so that Mordecai and Rigby could see what was on it. Mordecai couldn't believe his eyes. Sure enough, there was an email from him, saying all those horrible things to Benson! It was just like the text he'd "sent" to Margaret.

"Benson, you gotta believe me. I didn't . . . ," Mordecai said.

"I don't want to hear it. Go home. You're suspended without pay until further notice. You too, Rigby," Benson ordered.

"C'mon! I didn't do anything!" Rigby whined.

"You're lucky I'm not firing the two of you. Now, get out of here," Benson said.

Mordecai and Rigby walked back to their house. Rigby couldn't believe it! He totally needed that money for pizza later. Mordecai just stared at the ground and slumped his shoulders in defeat.

"Thanks a lot, dude. You wanna mess things up with Margaret, that's your deal. But messing with Benson so I get suspended, too? Weak sauce," Rigby said.

"Seriously?" was all Mordecai could say, too angry to think of a better comeback.

When Mordecai and Rigby finally made it back home, they flopped on the couch. "Dude, I didn't send those messages, Rigby," Mordecai explained.

"Yeah, I know. Sorry for my outburst, bro. But who would want to screw up your life like this?" Rigby asked.

There was a knock at the door. Mordecai answered it. On the porch stood a man in a suit, holding a clipboard.

"Are you Mordecai?" the man asked.

"Yeah," Mordecai said. "What's up?"

"My name is Tom, and I'm from the Vista Credit-Card Collection Agency. It shows here that you are behind on your payments. You owe us more than six million dollars."

Mordecai's mouth dropped open. "What? I don't have a credit card."

Tom nodded. "That's what they all say."

Mordecai threw up his hands, motioning around the house. "If I had six million dollars' worth of stuff, do you think I'd be living here? Working at a park?"

Tom handed Mordecai a piece of paper and turned to leave. "You have twenty-four hours to pay your bill. Thank you."

Mordecai stared at the piece of paper. How was he going to fix this, on top of everything else that happened?

"Dude! You have a Vista card, and six million dollars of stuff, and you never shared with me?!" Rigby said.

"C'mon, Rigby. We *just* talked about this."

"Oh yeah. Sorry, man. It still makes me wonder who would screw with you like this," Rigby said.

Then, out of nowhere, the TV turned itself on and a video-game version of Mordecai's face filled the screen. "It's me, Mordecai," the video-game version of Mordecai said.

Mordecai jumped up from the couch and stuck his face really close to the screen. "My gaming avatar? What's the deal? Why are doing this?!"

Avatar-Mordecai laughed. "You really don't know, do you? I want your life! I want your friends. And to do that, I must eliminate you!"

"But you're not even real!" Mordecai screamed back.

"Yet! Mwahahaha. I've already destroyed your 'real' life by hacking into all of your electronic devices, creating a fake credit card, and stealing your identity," Avatar-Mordecai answered calmly. "If you want your life back, you must defeat me in a challenge."

"Name it," Moredecai answered, with the focus of a ninja about to go into battle.

"You must win a game. A video game. A video game in which you undo all the things I've done to you," Avatar-Mordecai challenged. "But be warned: You have to play using me—your avatar—and I won't be controlled easily. You will have to defeat levels *and* defeat me."

Mordecai grabbed the game controller. "Whatever, dude. It's on!"

Avatar-Mordecai disappeared from the screen, and was replaced by the first level of *Money Grabber*, a game in which a player has to gather as many coins as possible. Rigby reached for the controls.

"Give it here, I hold the world record for this game," Rigby said. "I'll help you beat this guy!"

But before he could grab the controller, a bolt of electricity shot out and zapped Rigby's hand.

"Mordecai must complete this challenge by himself!" Avatar-Mordecai's voice echoed throughout the house. Mordecai nodded and began to play the game. He tried moving Avatar-Mordecai through the first level. But it wouldn't move.

"What? You won't even let me start?" Mordecai

said. Avatar-Mordecai didn't respond. Mordecai tried pushing the controller's buttons again. But nothing happened. He felt anger swelling up inside him. He was trapped in a game he couldn't possibly win.

Frustrated, he threw the controller to the floor and kicked it.

"It's hopeless!"

A message popped up on the screen: ENTER CODE.

"What?" Mordecai said, confused. "There isn't a code for this game."

Rigby smiled, "Yeah, but maybe the code will let you control your guy!"

"But what's the code?" Mordecai wondered, picking up the controller.

"Dude. It's *always* up, up, down, down, left, right, left, right, B, A, start. You know that!" Rigby said.

Mordecai pressed the buttons as Rigby suggested. The code message disappeared from the screen. Mordecai started moving his guy on the screen. The Avatar-Mordecai collected some coins. And then some more. Soon, he'd collected six hundred coins. This just might be possible . . .

Hours passed. Rigby's eyes were stuck wide open and dry as sand from watching Mordecai play for hours. He still was collecting coins. He was in the high five millions.

"What's the point of this?" Rigby asked tiredly.

Mordecai didn't respond. He was focused, but he looked like he was getting tired. On the screen, the Avatar-Mordecai jumped over a broken bridge and collected his six millionth coin. The game flashed and whistled. A new message appeared on the screen:

There was another knock at the door. Rigby answered and was surprised to see Vista Card Tom on the doorstep. He handed Rigby another piece of paper.

"Please give this form to Mordecai. Apparently there was an error, and he never had the debt. We apologize for the inconvenience," Tom said before he left.

"Epic," Rigby said. He returned to Mordecai, who had begun a new game: *Princess Save*.

Avatar-Mordecai was racing through numerous levels of the game. He had to defeat countless bad guys to rescue a princess. This game was long. It was difficult. And Mordecai knew he had to achieve victory.

Mordecai continued playing as Avatar-Mordecai.

Avatar-Mordecai was climbing up a steep hill, trying to reach the top where a massive castle stood. A large lion threw flaming barrels at Avatar-Mordecai. Avatar-Mordecai jumped out of the way, the barrel scorching the ground around him. Another barrel flew. And another. And another. The next one slammed into Avatar-Mordecai, catching him on fire for a second.

"Ow!" Mordecai said. The controller got too hot to handle. Mordecai picked it back up. "You're dead, castle lion!"

Avatar-Mordecai charged back up the hill, better able to dodge the flaming barrels.

"I think my avatar got hit on purpose!" Mordecai said. "How can I win if I can't even control my guy all the time?!"

This challenge was way intense—Mordecai needed some support from his best bro. Rigby couldn't play the games for Mordecai, but he could help in other ways.

Rigby scurried out of the house without Mordecai noticing—he was too busy trying to power up his avatar to get to the next level. Rigby ran all the way to the Coffee Shop, where he found Margaret and Eileen and began explaining everything to them.

Avatar-Mordecai struggled to swim through a lava pit. He was so close. He just had to get across the pit, climb the vine, and use the flaming sword of destiny on the King Lion to rescue the princess.

Slowly he climbed out of the lava pit and climbed the vine. A moment later he was face-to-face with the dreaded King Lion. He pulled the flaming sword of destiny from behind him and swung at the King Lion. A pixilated rainbow of fire flew at the King Lion, disintegrating him.

"Yes!" Mordecai yelled.

Avatar-Mordecai charged toward the princess and unlocked her from her cell.

ACHIEVEMENT UNLOCKED: APOLOGY TO MARGARET SENT.

"Whatever, Rigby. That is the most ridiculous thing I've ever heard," Margaret said.

Her phone vibrated. It was a text from a number she didn't recognize. MORDECAI DIDN'T SEND THAT TEXT.

Margaret looked at Rigby, stunned. "It's the truth?! I've got to help him!"

Rigby smiled. "Bring coffee."

Rigby had another errand to run. He ran straight from the Coffee Shop to Benson's office, where Benson was still sitting behind his desk, fuming about Mordecai's email. Before Benson could throw him out, Rigby explained everything that had happened. Benson picked up his emergency Park phone and called the rest of the staff, telling them to go to the house and support Mordecai however they could.

"Nobody threatens me with chewing and gets away with it!" Benson said, slamming the door to his office on his way out.

When Rigby walked through the front door of his house, the scene in the living room looked a lot different than how he had left it. Mordecai was sweating profusely. Behind him, Muscle Man stood rubbing Mordecai's shoulders and shouting, "You're the boss! You're the king!"

Eileen poured cup of coffee after cup of coffee and handed them to Margaret, who handed them to Mordecai. Mordecai

slammed each cup down his throat without taking his eyes off the screen. He was focused on another part of the game, in which Avatar-Mordecai had to pop thousands of bubble-gum bubbles, using whatever he could find in the background—lasers, arrows, sticks. Benson just stood there, glaring at the screen. In the background, Skips stood silently. Watching.

"Almost . . . there . . . ," Mordecai said, popping bubble after bubble. And then . . .

Music blasted from the TV! Mordecai had popped all the bubbles.

ACHIEVEMENT UNLOCKED: CORRECTING EMAIL SENT TO BENSON.

Benson continued glaring at the screen. "Popping bubble-gum bubbles doesn't seem like much of an apology!"

Avatar-Mordecai appeared on the screen.

"Well done, Mordecai," Avatar-Mordecai said. "You reversed all the things I did with your identity. But you haven't completed the challenge quite yet. I actually never wanted your life. I don't care about you or your loser friends. I just wanted to make you pay for destroying me in the past!"

Avatar-Mordecai morphed on the screen and became the Destroyer of Worlds!

"If you want your life back, you will have to defeat me again! But that's impossible! Hahahahahahahaha!" Destroyer of Worlds screamed in evil laughter.

"You're finished, Destroyer! You thought you could destroy my life, except my friends know me better than that. You can't destroy my world, but I'm gonna destroy yours once and for all!"

Mordecai nodded at Skips. Skips tossed Mordecai an upgraded version of the Maximum Glove. It was like the old Maximum Glove, but with more buttons and controls. Mordecai punched a code into the glove.

"I knew it was you when you said I had to beat a video game. And I know how to beat it. While I was playing, I had Skips here program an enhanced version of Lemon Chef into the Ultra Maximum Glove," Mordecai said, defiant.

On the TV screen, Ultra Lemon Chef pixilated into existence. Like the original Lemon Chef, he was made up of different video-game parts. Only this time he was bigger, stronger, and faster, made up of parts from every video game in existence.

Mordecai swung the Ultra Maximum Glove, causing Ultra Lemon Chef to smash a fist into Destroyer of World's face. The Destroyer reeled backwards. Mordecai extended his arm. Ultra Lemon Chef copied the motion, and fired a blast of video-game energy at Destroyer of Worlds. The devilish video-game villain exploded in a colorful display of pixels.

The TV went dark. Mordecai had won! He jumped up from the couch and cheered. His friends all cheered and danced around him. Margaret dumped hot coffee over her own head in celebration. Talk about an awesome victory!

"Thanks for your help and support, everyone," Mordecai said once the commotion had died down. "I couldn't have done it without each and every one of you."

"You can always count on your friends, dude," Rigby said.

"And my friends can always count on me," Mordecai said. "Now let's order some pizza and play some video games to relax!"